Dramasc

CW01597060

Three Classic Thrillers

Adapted by
JOHN O'CONNOR

With explanatory notes and activities by
JOHN O'CONNOR

Nelson

Thomas Nelson & Sons Ltd
Nelson House
Mayfield Road
Walton-on-Thames
Surrey KT12 5PL
United Kingdom

The Signal-Man; The Monkey's Paw; The Canterville Ghost – the scripts © John O'Connor 1999.
The right of John O'Connor to be identified as author of these plays has been asserted by John O'Connor in accordance with Copyright, Design and Patents Act 1988.
The Monkey's Paw adapted with permission obtained from The Society of Authors as the Literary Representative of the Estate of W. W. Jacobs.
All applications to perform these plays should be addressed in the first instance to the Royalty and Permissions Department, ITPS Ltd, Cheriton House, North Way, Andover, Hampshire SP10 5BE (Telephone 01264 342756; Fax 01264 342792).

Introduction, activities and explanatory notes © Thomas Nelson 1999

Designed and produced by Bender Richardson White
Edited by Elizabeth Paren
Typesetting by Malcolm Smythe
Cover illustration by Dave Grimwood
Black and white illustrations by John James
Printed by Zrinski Printing and Publishing House, Čakovec, Croatia

This edition published by Thomas Nelson & Sons Ltd 1999
ISBN 0–17–432598–3
9 8 7 6 5 4 3 2 1
03 02 01 00 99

All rights reserved. No part of this publication may be reproduced, copied or transmitted in any form or by any means, electronic or mechanical, including photocopy, recording, or any information storage and retrieval system, without permission in writing from the publisher or under license from the Copyright Licensing Authority Ltd., 90 Tottenham Court Road, London W1P 9HE.

Contents

Series Editor's Introduction

Dramascripts is an exciting series of plays especially chosen for students in the lower and middle years of secondary school. The titles range from the best in modern writing to adaptations of classic texts such as *A Christmas Carol* and *Silas Marner*.

Dramascripts can be read or acted purely for the enjoyment and stimulation that they provide; however, each play in the series also offers all the support that pupils need in working with the text in the classroom:

- **Introduction** – this offers important background information and explains something about the ways in which the play came to be written.
- **Script** – this is clearly set out in ways that make the play easy to handle in the classroom.
- **Notes** explain references that pupils might not understand, and language points that are not obvious.
- **Activities** – at the end of scenes, acts or sections – give pupils the opportunity to explore the play more fully. Types of activity include: discussion, writing, hot-seating, improvisation, acting, freeze-framing, story-boarding and artwork.
- **Looking Back at the Play** – this section has further activities for more extended work on the play as a whole with emphasis on characters, plots, themes and language.

INTRODUCTION

The plays in this anthology are adaptations of three of the finest short stories in the English language, each offering its own perspective on the world of the supernatural.

Charles Dickens's *The Signal-Man* is a macabre tale, its setting an isolated signal-box situated between the dark and forbidding cliffs of a remote railway cutting; in *The Monkey's Paw*, W.W. Jacobs demonstrates the inexorable cruelty of fate as it affects a simple working couple and their only son; while Oscar Wilde's *The Canterville Ghost* contrives to be both farcical and poignant as it presents the confrontation between New-World scepticism and the traditions of the country-house haunting.

Individually these are ideal classroom plays, with fast-moving plots and intriguing mysteries; together they offer insights into the supernatural story genre, as practised by three of its masters.

Dramascripts

The Signal-Man

CHARLES DICKENS

Adapted by
JOHN O'CONNOR

CHARLES DICKENS

Possibly the most famous British writer after Shakespeare, Charles Dickens was born in Portsmouth in 1812, the son of a clerk in the navy office. His father was a good-natured man, but often owed money, and when he was imprisoned for debt, Charles was taken out of school at the age of twelve and forced to work in a shoe-blacking factory sticking labels to bottles. He later used memories of this painful time in some of his novels, especially *David Copperfield.* When he was fifteen he became a House of Commons reporter and began to write a series of comic descriptions later published as *Sketches by Boz.* He then achieved great success with *The Pickwick Papers* and was famous in Britain and America by the age of 24. The series of works which followed – including *A Christmas Carol, Oliver Twist,* and *Great Expectations* – made Dickens the most popular of all English novelists and he was mourned throughout the world when he died of a stroke in 1870, aged 58.

The Scenes

Scene 1 The railway tunnel
Scene 2 The railway tunnel
Scene 3 The signal-box
Scene 4 The railway tunnel

Staging

If played upon a traditional stage, one end could show a representation of the tunnel entrance, the other the interior of a signal-box.

THE CHARACTERS

SIGNAL-MAN

VISITOR

SPECTRE

ENGINE-DRIVER

RAILWAY-MAN

other railway-men and passengers

The Signal-Man

Scene 1

It is 1866. The stage is dark, and the only sounds are the moaning of the wind and the intermittent call of some night-bird. Then a single spot fades up to reveal a figure, and we hear the accompanying sound of a steam train, travelling at some speed. The figure has its back to us and is clearly being jolted by the movement of the train, but we can see enough to tell that he is a working man and is powerfully agitated about something, as he is making desperate waving movements with his right arm. Suddenly there is a horrendous screeching noise – the train is applying its brakes – the man seems to shield his eyes with his left hand, while gesticulating even more frenziedly with his right, and – just as the metallic din grows unbearably loud – the stage is once more plunged into silence and blackness.

SCENE 2

Breaking the silence is an echoing sound of water dripping, as though in some cave or – as it turns out – a railway tunnel. The dim glow of a lantern appears from off stage and grows brighter until its bearer enters, treading carefully over the railway sleepers and holding his railway-man's lamp aloft, craning to see into the murky depths of this threatening blackness. It could be a routine check . . . were it not for the look of unmitigated horror etched into every feature . . . The lights dim as he stands rooted to the spot, gazing straight out ahead.

ARTWORK: Imagine that you are making a film version of The Signal-Man. Storyboard Scenes 1 and 2 in five or six frames. The first frame might look like this:

ARTWORK: Draw an illustration or a sketch-plan of the set, based either on the stage directions to Scene 1, or your own idea of what would be practical and interesting.

SCENE 3

The lights come up on the warm glow of a signal-box: wood panelling; rows of levers; bells, flags, railway manuals, timetables; and a row of windows which look out on to the damp and gloomy walls of a steep railway cutting.

A kettle is whistling on the hob, and a man dressed like a hiker (and who appears to have been carrying the heavy rucksack which lies open by the door) is hastily pouring tea from a brown tea-pot into a very large mug. He looks concernedly off stage, adds a dash of brandy from a hip-flask, and calls out, in as reassuring a tone as he can muster.

VISITOR Come back in. I do assure you: there's no-one out there.

(The SIGNAL-MAN enters, extinguishes and hangs up his lamp, and sits shivering in his windsor chair. The VISITOR wraps a grey blanket round the SIGNAL-MAN's shoulders and places the mug of tea in his trembling hands.)

Here. Drink this.

SIGNAL-MAN Thank you, sir. *(He drinks, coughs, and wipes his mouth with the edge of the blanket.)* Thank you. You must excuse my strange behaviour, sir, I . . .

(The SIGNAL-MAN breaks off, as though needing to compose himself, and takes another gulp of tea.)

VISITOR I was on the footpath at the top of the cutting and saw you coming out of the tunnel. Was there something inside it which had alarmed you? *(The SIGNAL-MAN does not reply, but takes another mouthful of tea.)* Or was it when I called out to you? I simply wanted to know the best way down . . . The cutting is steep-sided and I did not wish to sprain my ankle . . . That is why I called out . . .

SIGNAL-MAN *(Suddenly reacting to his visitor's questions.)* But why did you call out 'Halloa! Below there!' Why those particular words?

VISITOR Did I call that? It was certainly something to that effect . . .

SIGNAL-MAN Not to that effect, sir. Those were the very words. I know them well.

VISITOR All right. Admitting those were the very words, I said them no doubt because I saw you below.

SIGNAL-MAN For no other reason?

VISITOR What other reason could I possibly have?

SIGNAL-MAN You had no feeling that they were conveyed to you in any supernatural way?

VISITOR Of course not. You look at me *(Forcing a smile.)* as if you had a dread of me.

SIGNAL-MAN I was doubtful . . . whether I had seen you before.

VISITOR Where?

(The SIGNAL-MAN looks off stage in the direction of the tunnel, frightened.)

By the tunnel?

(He looks at his visitor intently and silently nods.)

My good fellow, I have never even visited this county before. I am on a walking holiday, on my way to stay with a friend a few miles north of here. And what should I do by your tunnel? I have never been here in my life, you may swear.

SIGNAL-MAN *(Sighing.)* I think I may . . . Yes, I am sure I may.

(The warning bell sounds. The SIGNAL-MAN forces himself to rise and answer it, pulls one of the heavy levers, and then stares out of the cabin window.)

VISITOR You must certainly have mistaken me for someone else . . . Who, do you think?

SIGNAL-MAN *(Turning back, after a pause.)* I don't know.

VISITOR Someone you know?

SIGNAL-MAN No.

VISITOR But like me?

SIGNAL-MAN I don't know. I've never seen the face. The left arm is across his eyes and the right is waved – violently waved – like this.

(He imitates the actions of the man seen in the first scene, his left arm across his face and his right arm waving wildly.)

VISITOR *(Thoughtfully.)* As though he were crying out *(Struggling to find exactly the right words.)* . . . 'For God's sake, clear the way!'?

warning bell *The bell to alert the signal-man either that a train is approaching or that it is time to change the points on the line by means of one of the levers.*

SIGNAL-MAN I hadn't put it into words myself, sir . . . But, yes. Yes. 'For God's sake, clear the way!'

VISITOR Tell me your story.

(He hands him the hip-flask and the SIGNAL-MAN takes a substantial swig before summoning the courage to continue.)

SIGNAL-MAN One moonlit night I was sitting here, when I heard a voice cry: 'Halloa! Below there!'. . .

(The lights cross-fade from the signal-box to the tunnel entrance, where we see the SPECTRE, just as the SIGNAL-MAN describes, dressed in a railway-man's outfit, like the SIGNAL-MAN's own, his arm obscuring his face. The SIGNAL-MAN's narrative continues in recorded 'voice-over', as we watch the re-enactment of his story, the actor having simply moved from one end of the stage to the other, and the fading up of howling wind helping to create the ghostly, unsettling atmosphere of the flashback. The dialogue in the flashback can be spoken simultaneously with the voice-over, or mimed.)

I started up, looked from that door, and saw this Someone Else standing by the red light near the tunnel, waving as I just now showed you. The voice seemed hoarse with shouting, and it cried: 'Look out! Look out!' I snatched my lamp, turned it on red, and ran towards the figure, calling, 'What's wrong? What has happened? Where?' It stood just outside the blackness of the tunnel. I advanced so close upon it that I wondered at its keeping the sleeve across its eyes. I ran right up at it, and had my hand stretched out to pull the sleeve away . . . when it was gone.

(A second's sudden black-out and silence, during which we hear the visitor's question.)

VISITOR Into the tunnel?

(The lights quickly fade up on the signal-box, the SIGNAL-MAN now standing by the door looking out in the direction of the tunnel, the VISITOR sitting in the chair.)

SIGNAL-MAN No. I ran on into the tunnel, five hundred yards. I stopped, and held my lamp above my head, and saw the figures of the measured distance, and saw the wet stains stealing down the walls and trickling through the arch. I ran out again faster than I had run in – for I had a mortal abhorrence of the place upon me – and I looked all round the red light at the tunnel entrance, and I went up the iron ladder to the gallery atop of it, and I came back here. I telegraphed both ways: 'An alarm has been given. Is anything wrong?' The answer came back, both ways: 'All well.'

VISITOR Then surely this figure must have been a deception of your sight. It has been known for people to be troubled by visions which originate purely in a mis-function of the delicate nerves that minister to the eye . . . And, as to an imaginary cry, do but listen for a moment to the wind in this unnatural valley while we speak so low, and to the wild harp it makes on the telegraph wires.

SIGNAL-MAN That's all very well. I ought to know something of the wind and the wires – I who have so often passed long winter nights here, alone and watching. But there is something else . . .

VISITOR Yes?

SIGNAL-MAN It happened within six hours of the Appearance . . .

the figures of the measured distance *Numbers were painted on the tunnel walls to let railway workers know how far into the tunnel they had come.*

a mortal abhorrence *A terrible dread, as though it were a threat to his life.*

which originate purely in a mis-function . . . *The visitor tries to persuade the signal-man that the vision was due to something wrong with his eyes.*

(During this speech, we hear the sound of an express train and its distant whistle, which becomes louder as the SIGNAL-MAN speaks.)

The express was due – the night train from the north – and I had received a message that the line was clear. I walked down to the track and held my green light aloft as it roared past into the tunnel . . . And then, just as I turned back, and was climbing the steps to my box, I heard it . . .

(The steam train sounds convert to the hideous metallic grating heard in Scene 1, but this time they climax in the terrifying noises of a crash, followed by the screams of injured and bewildered passengers. The lights fade up on the tunnel entrance and we see the scenes of destruction, as the wounded and the dead are carried out on stretchers, or helped out, limping. Their words are obscured by the howling wind, but the reaction of the VISITOR is heard in voice-over.)

VISITOR Of course. The Mugby Tunnel Tragedy. I didn't realise . . .

(. . . as the lights cross-fade from the tunnel scene back to the signal-box.)

SIGNAL-MAN No. There's no sign to tell you where you are; no monument to record the site of the disaster, as it happened well inside the tunnel.

VISITOR How dreadful! But you continued working here?

SIGNAL-MAN Yes. I was not to blame. But there is more.

VISITOR More?

SIGNAL-MAN Yes. That all happened just a year ago. Six or seven months passed and I had recovered from the shock, when one

my green light *To show that the way ahead was clear.*

morning, as the day was breaking and I was standing at the door, looking towards the red light, I saw the spectre again.

(He stops, with a fixed look at the VISITOR.)

VISITOR Did it cry out?

SIGNAL-MAN No. It was silent.

VISITOR Did it wave its arm?

SIGNAL-MAN No. It leaned against the shaft of light, with both hands before the face, like this.

(He takes up a position sometimes seen on war monuments, mourning the loss of those who have fallen in battle, the head bowed, both hands crossed in front of the face.)

VISITOR Did you go up to it?

SIGNAL-MAN I came in and sat down, partly to collect my thoughts, partly because it had turned me faint. When I went to the door again, daylight was above me, and the ghost was gone.

VISITOR But nothing followed? Nothing came of this?

(The SIGNAL-MAN stares ahead, as though in a trance, and we hear the clickety-clack sounds that a passenger would hear from their seat in a carriage, as he tells the story.)

SIGNAL-MAN That very day, as a train came out of the tunnel, I noticed, at a carriage window on my side, what looked like a confusion of hands and heads, and something waved.

(Over the train sounds there comes a sudden and violent scream of a woman, and then silence.)

I saw it just in time to change the signal to stop, and the driver put his brake on, but the train drifted past here, a hundred and fifty yards or more. I ran after it, and, as I went along, I heard terrible cries. A beautiful young woman had been killed in one of the compartments. She was brought in here, and laid down on this floor between us.

(They both look down and the VISITOR involuntarily pushes his chair back, momentarily lost for words. In the pause which follows, we become aware of the moaning wind outside and the uncanny whistling of the wires. Then the SIGNAL-MAN braces himself for the final part of his disturbing narrative.)

Now, sir, mark this, and judge how my mind is troubled. Ever since, it has been there, now and again, by fits and starts.

VISITOR At the light?

SIGNAL-MAN At the Danger-light.

VISITOR What does it do?

(He does not speak, but repeats that same gesticulation of 'For God's sake, clear the way!')

SIGNAL-MAN I have no peace or rest for it. It calls to me, for many minutes together, in an agonised manner: 'Below there! Look out! Look out!' It stands waving to me. It rings my warning bell . . .

VISITOR Your bell?

SIGNAL-MAN Yes, sir. *(Then, trying to control his voice.)* It has rung twice since you have been sitting in that chair.

VISITOR But that cannot be possible – I would have heard it. I assure you that your imagination is misleading you. My eyes have been on that bell and my ears open to it; and, if I am a living man, it has not sounded – except, of course, when it was rung in the natural course of physical things by the station communicating with you.

SIGNAL-MAN *(Shaking his head.)* I have never made a mistake as to that yet, sir. I have never confused the spectre's ring with the man's. The ghost's ring is a strange vibration in the bell that it derives from nothing else. And I have not asserted that the bell stirs to the eye. I don't wonder that you failed to hear it. But *I* heard it.

VISITOR I recall you going to the door while we were talking. Was it in answer to the bell's ring?

SIGNAL-MAN It was.

VISITOR And did the spectre seem to be there when you looked out?

SIGNAL-MAN It was there.

VISITOR Both times?

SIGNAL-MAN *(Firmly.)* Both times.

VISITOR Will you come to the door with me and look for it now?

(The VISITOR gets up, walks to the door and looks out, but the SIGNAL-MAN remains motionless in his chair.)

SIGNAL-MAN What do you see?

VISITOR I see the Danger-light and the dismal mouth of the tunnel. I see the high, wet, stone walls of the cutting, and the stars above them.

SIGNAL-MAN Nothing else?

VISITOR No.

(The SIGNAL-MAN joins him by the door.)

SIGNAL-MAN *(Sighing with relief.)* No. It is not there.

VISITOR Agreed.

(They go back to their seats and the SIGNAL-MAN picks up the conversation as though they had been discussing a subject of undisputed fact.)

SIGNAL-MAN By this time you will fully understand, sir, that what

I have not asserted that the bell stirs to the eye *The bell does not appear to move when it rings.*

troubles me so dreadfully is the question 'What does the spectre mean?'

VISITOR I am not sure I follow you.

SIGNAL-MAN *(Staring into the fire, and only occasionally looking up at his VISITOR.)* What is it warning against? What is the danger? Where is the danger? There is danger overhanging somewhere on the line. Some dreadful calamity will happen. It is not to be doubted this third time, after what has gone before. But surely this is a cruel haunting of me. What can I do? *(He pulls out his handkerchief to wipe the perspiration from his forehead.)* If I telegraph 'Danger' on either side of me, or both, I can give no reason for it. *(Now wiping the palms of his hands.)* I should get into trouble and do no good. They would think I was mad.

VISITOR Oh, surely not. They . . .

SIGNAL-MAN Yes, sir, this is the way it would work: message – 'Danger! Take care'; answer – 'What danger? Where?'; message – 'Don't know. But, for God's sake, take care!' They would displace me. What else could they do?

(He stands and pushes his hair from off his gleaming forehead, now feverish in the extremity of his distress.)

When it first stood under the Danger-light, why didn't it tell me where that accident was to happen – if it must happen? Why not tell me if it could be averted – if it could have been averted? When, on its second coming, it hid its face, why not tell me, instead: 'She is going to die. Let them keep her at home'? If it came, on those two occasions, only to show me that its warnings were true, and so prepare me for the third, why not warn me plainly now? And I, Lord

now feverish . . . *The signal-man is running a temperature and sweating in his confusion about what to do.*

help me! A mere poor signal-man on this solitary posting! Why not go to somebody with credit to be believed and power to act?

VISITOR *(Struggling to find some words with which to comfort him.)* I cannot answer your questions. I can only say that it should be some comfort to you to know that you discharge your duty faithfully and conscientiously – even if you do not understand these confounding Appearances.

(The bell sounds and both men start. But this is an earthly ringing and the SIGNAL-MAN rises to answer it and activate two levers.)

(Getting up.) Will you do something for me?

SIGNAL-MAN What is that, sir?

VISITOR Allow me to keep you company here during your shift tonight.

SIGNAL-MAN No, sir, thank you. Apart from other considerations, it would break all regulations. But I appreciate your offer.

VISITOR Something else then. I told you I was about to stay with a friend in the county. He is a doctor. Will you at least come with me and let him hear your story? I am still of the opinion that the desolation of this wild and gloomy spot, together with the shock of those two dreadful catastrophes on the line, might have . . .

SIGNAL-MAN Unbalanced my mind?

VISITOR Made it easier for you to imagine things. Will you do as I ask?

SIGNAL-MAN Very well. But I know that no doctor will ease my agitation.

with credit to be believed *The railway company would only believe someone in a powerful or more senior position than the signal-man.*

And no one will convince me that what I have seen is the workings of my imagination or the effects of a misfunctioning eyesight.

VISITOR *(Standing and shaking the SIGNAL-MAN's hand.)* Good night. I shall return for you when your shift ends, at . . . ?

SIGNAL-MAN Eleven tomorrow morning, sir. The relief man will do the day-shift.

VISITOR Until eleven then.

(He leaves and the SIGNAL-MAN stands by the open door, watching him climb the walls of the cutting. Suddenly he stiffens and the expression of terror comes back, as he slowly turns and stares in horror at the bell, which, though quite still, is now sounding in a hollow, ghostly ring, quite unlike the business-like clatter we have heard before. He claps his hands to his ears and swings round to face the door. As the lights dim, he prepares himself once more to look upon the SPECTRE which – he is certain of it – will be standing under the Danger-light by the tunnel entrance.)

(In the blackout, the ghostly bell continues to ring.)

INTERVIEWING AND WRITING: Imagine that it is the day after the terrible Mugby Tunnel rail-crash. Interview the signal-man, asking him exactly what happened. Then write a newspaper article on the accident, using the information that he has provided, as well as any other facts you might wish to add.

ACTING: Act out the sequence where the signal-man tells the visitor about the death of the young woman (from 'That very day . . .' (line 163) to . . . *his disturbing narrative.*), bringing out the signal-man's horror and the visitor's reactions to the story.

ARTWORK: Draw a sketch of the signal-man's view from the door of the signal-box at a moment when the spectre has appeared in the tunnel entrance.

IMPROVISATION: Improvise a scene in which the signal-man explains his dilemma (about not being able to warn anyone) and the visitor advises him on what he ought to do.

WRITING: Annotate the script from 'But that cannot be possible . . . ' (line 194) to the end of the scene, to show the visitor's developing thoughts and changing feelings. How does he react to the signal-man's strange tale and disturbing behaviour? Add notes such as 'I will try to reassure him ...' or 'What can I say?'

WRITING: Write the visitor's diary entry for that night, when he has a chance to reflect upon the disturbing experience of meeting the signal-man and the strange tale that he has heard.

DISCUSSION: Predict how the story will end. What is the meaning behind the spectre's appearance? Does the spectre represent anyone in particular (such as Death, or the signal-man himself, or the visitor, or an unknown person)? What might the third tragedy be? Discuss what part might be played by the particular words: 'Halloa! Below there!' and 'For God's sake, clear the way!'

SCENE 4

The next morning. A single spot illuminates a man like the figure at the beginning of the story, this time facing us, and gesticulating in complete silence. From the darkness off stage, we hear the voice of the VISITOR, calling out anxiously.

VISITOR *(Off stage.)* What's the matter?

(The lights come up to show that the gesticulating man is standing amongst a group of four others, all railwaymen by their dress, and, as the VISITOR joins them, panting from the difficult descent of the cutting, the man drops his arm and is comforted by one of his friends.)

What has happened?

RAILWAY-MAN Signal-man killed this morning, sir.

VISITOR Not the man who worked that box?

RAILWAY-MAN Yes, sir

VISITOR Not the man I know?

RAILWAY-MAN You will recognise him, sir, if you knew him, for his face is quite composed.

(The men move apart to reveal a tarpaulin, covering a body. One pulls back the portion of the cloth covering the dead man's face and the VISITOR looks at it, nodding slowly.)

VISITOR O, how did this happen? How did this happen?

RAILWAY-MAN He was cut down by an engine, sir. No man in England knew his work better. But somehow he was not clear of the rails. He had extinguished the light and had the lamp in his hand. As the engine came out of the tunnel, his back was towards her, and she cut him down. That man drove her, and was showing how it happened. Show the gentleman, Tom.

(The man who had been waving steps forward, helped by his friend, clearly still in some distress.)

ENGINE-DRIVER Coming round the curve in the tunnel, sir, I saw him at the end, like as if I saw him down a telescope. There was no time to check speed, and I knew him to be very careful. As he didn't seem to take heed of the whistle, I shut it off when we were running down upon him, and called to him as loud as I could call.

VISITOR *(Almost unable to utter the question.)* What did you say?

ENGINE-DRIVER I said: 'Halloa! Below there!' And then: 'For God's sake, clear the way!'

VISITOR *(To himself, in whispered horror.)* 'For God's sake, clear the way!'

ENGINE-DRIVER Ah! It was a dreadful time, sir. I never left off calling to him. I put this arm before my eyes, as I couldn't bear to see, and I waved this arm to the last. *(He repeats the familiar actions.)* . . . But it was no use . . . I did my best, sir. I kept calling to the last: 'For God's sake, clear the way! For God's sake, clear the way!'. . . Are you all right, sir?

(The VISITOR does not answer, but simply stares into the depths of that ominous tunnel.)

FREEZE-FRAME: Freeze-frame the opening of Scene 4 at the point where the visitor enters to see the distressed railwayman standing in front of the tunnel, demonstrating what he had seen to the others.

ARTWORK: Draw a time-line to show when the spectre was seen and what followed.

WRITING: Imagine that the signal-man had been writing his own story, which is found in the signal-box after his death. Write the final few pages, in which he recounts the recent strange experiences and concludes with the day's visit from a hiker.

DISCUSSION: Discuss the ending and explain exactly what has happened in your opinion. In particular, show how the spectre, the visitor and the engine-driver were all somehow involved in the signal-man's death.

WRITING: Write another newspaper article, in which you refer to the fact that this is the third tragedy to take place on the line in recent months. Include quotations from everybody concerned, including the visitor and the engine-driver.

Dramascripts

The Monkey's Paw

W. W. Jacobs

Adapted by

John O'Connor

W. W. JACOBS

Like Dickens, William Wymark Jacobs was born near the docks, in this case Wapping in London, where his father worked as a labourer loading ships. His first job was as a clerk in the civil service, but he quickly began to have short stories published in popular periodicals, including the *Strand Magazine*, where Conan Doyle's Sherlock Holmes adventures also appeared. He became a full-time writer in 1896, after the success of *Many Cargoes*, his first collection of short stories, and then wrote a number of novels. He is mainly known as a writer of short stories, however, including the extremely funny escapades of a country rogue called Bob Pretty, and many stories of the macabre, of which *The Monkey's Paw* is justifiably the most famous. He died in 1943.

The Scenes

Scene 1 Tropical forest, India
Scene 2 The living room, Laburnam Villa, evening
Scene 3 The living room, Laburnam Villa, the next morning
Scene 4 The living room, Laburnam Villa, ten days later

Staging

Apart from Scene 1, which does not require scenery (sound-effects establishing the location), the play is set in the parlour of a small, working-class terraced house in the suburbs of a provincial town in Edwardian England. There is a front door and a window, both looking out on to the garden path and the street beyond, and an open staircase against the side wall, leading up to the bedrooms on the first floor. In the opposite wall there is a fireplace and mantelpiece. Apart from the usual furniture, there is an upright piano in the corner.

Music

Music could be played between each scene. This could be either something Edwardian, or possibly Indian sitar music.

THE CHARACTERS

ALFRED WHITE *a retired workman; late 60s.*

ELSIE WHITE *his wife; the same age.*

HERBERT WHITE *their son; 30.*

SERGEANT-MAJOR MORRIS *an old soldier; late 60s.*

CORPORAL MASTERSON *a soldier serving in India.*

MR ROBINSON *from Meggins Manufactory.*

The Monkey's Paw

Scene 1

Darkness. And the shrill sound – quiet at first, but slowly and insistently building – of the tropical forest: birds, monkeys and strange insects. After a second or two, another sound – the low moaning of a human being in some terrible agony.

A solitary spot fades up to illuminate a man, dressed in a Victorian soldier's tropical gear, lying on the forest floor and writhing in torment. Suddenly he forces himself to a sitting position and, as though remembering something on which his life depends, he jerks his trembling hands towards his tunic and pulls some small object out of the top pocket. Though still shaking, a calm descends upon him and he now seems possessed by some terrible resolve. Staring wildly at the object in his hand, his speech clears for the first time to enable him to utter his final intelligible sentence.

MASTERSON Death! I wish for death!

(He screams, and flings the object to the ground, squirming away from it in terror, as though it had assumed a life of its own as he held it in his hand for the last time. Then, after a long, exhausted sigh, he leans back and closes his eyes.)

MORRIS *(Off stage.)* Masterson! Masterson!

(The owner of the voice enters, another soldier we will later recognise as MORRIS. Seeing his comrade, he flings his rifle to the ground and kneels next to him, trying desperately to force some water between the lips of the dying man. But MASTERSON pushes the flask away, his eyes now staring wildly, and, in a voice which hints at some unspeakable terror, whispers his dying words.)

possessed by some terrible resolve *As though frighteningly controlled by a determination to do something.*

MASTERSON The paw, Morris! The monkey's paw!

(MORRIS gently lowers the dead man to the ground and closes his glaring eyes. He stands, picks up his rifle and is about to leave when he turns, staring back at a spot on the ground near MASTERSON's body. Then, as though making a decision, he strides back, snatches the paw from the ground, places it in the top pocket of his tunic, and, with a final pitying look at MASTERSON, leaves the clearing.)

ACTING AND DISCUSSION: Act out Scene 1 and then discuss what you think has happened to Masterson and what the significance of the monkey's paw might be.

SCENE 2

Evening in the living room (or 'parlour') of Laburnam Villa, a small terraced house in the suburbs. The wind and rain can occasionally be heard beating on the window, but the room is cosy enough, with the curtains drawn and a fire burning brightly.
MR WHITE and his son HERBERT are playing chess; MRS WHITE is sitting by the fire knitting – and occasionally acting as peace-maker in some of the disputes which arise over the chess-board.

Pleased at spotting an exciting move, HERBERT delightedly pushes a piece into a threatening position. MR WHITE sees the danger and, to distract his opponent, tries to engage him in conversation about the weather as he moves his king . . .

MR WHITE Hark at the wind.

HERBERT *(Grimly surveying the board and executing another move.)* Check!

MR WHITE *(Hand poised over the board.)* I should hardly think he'd come tonight.

HERBERT *(Satisfyingly, as he responds to his father's move.)* Mate!

MR WHITE *(With a sudden loss of temper.)* That's the worst of living so far out. Of all the beastly, slushy, out-of-the-way places to live in, this is the worst. Path's a bog and the road's a torrent. I don't know what people are thinking about. I suppose because only two houses in the road are let, they think it doesn't matter.

check . . . mate *Chess-players say 'check' to announce that the opponent's king is under threat; in a further move, 'mate' means that the king is 'dead' and the game over.*

only two houses in the road are let *Most of the houses in the street are rented out, but all except two are empty.*

MRS WHITE *(Soothingly.)* Never mind, dear: perhaps you'll win the next one.

(MR WHITE looks up sharply, just in time to intercept a knowing smile between mother and son, and hides a guilty grin in his thin grey beard. The sound of the garden gate is heard, as it swings closed, followed by heavy footsteps approaching the door.)

MR WHITE There he is!

(He opens the door and lets MORRIS in, wet and cold from his journey. As the two men greet each other, HERBERT places the best chair by the fire and MRS WHITE hangs the Sergeant-Major's coat on a peg under the stairs.)

Come in, Morris, come in. *(To his wife.)* My dear, this is the Sergeant-Major I told you about. Morris, this is my wife Elsie, and my son Herbert.

MORRIS I'm pleased to meet you all. Thank you for inviting me.

HERBERT How do you do, sir.

MRS WHITE You're very welcome. *(As MORRIS sits and gratefully accepts the tumbler of whisky that MR WHITE has poured for him.)* So you were with Alfred in the army?

MORRIS Only briefly. Our paths crossed in Aldershot.

MR WHITE But I returned home to domestic bliss, while you made your fortune in the mysterious east!

MORRIS *(Laughing.)* Not a fortune, White, but a good career in Her Majesty's forces.

HERBERT *(Excitedly: he has been eagerly awaiting the old soldier's visit.)* Tell us about India, sir.

> **Aldershot** *A major army centre and barracks.*
>
> **domestic bliss** *An expression meaning 'happiness in the home' here used comically.*

MR WHITE I'm afraid I made the mistake of telling Herbert some of those stories you were telling me the other day – you remember? *(Chuckling.)* The Maharajah's lost elephant . . . !

HERBERT Did you really recapture it yourself, sir?

MORRIS *(Smiling broadly at the memory.)* Not exactly single-handedly, Herbert. *(MR WHITE smiles at MORRIS and refills his tumbler.)* But I can describe my part in the escapade if you're really interested . . .

HERBERT Interested!

MORRIS And if Mrs White will forgive a soldier's reminiscences.

MRS WHITE It will be fascinating, Mr Morris. We get little enough in the way of romance and magic, living out here.

MORRIS Well, all right, then. Where should I begin, White?

MR WHITE With the elephant?

MORRIS The elephant. Well . . . *(Taking a fortifying mouthful of whisky.)* First there are one or two things you need to know about elephants . . .

(Music covers the rest of his speech and, as he gets under way, HERBERT especially hanging on every word, the lights dim to blackout.)

(After a few bars, the lights fade up again. A perceptive observer would notice that the clock has advanced by an hour and that the whisky bottle is almost empty . . . It also seems that the company has become less jolly, as MORRIS's stories have grown increasingly serious . . . There is a silence, during which MR WHITE looks at MORRIS.)

Maharajah *Head of one of India's royal families.*

MR WHITE Thirty-one years of it. When he left school, he was a slip of a youth. Now look at him.

MRS WHITE He don't look to have taken much harm.

MR WHITE I'd like to go to India myself. Just to look around a bit, you know.

MORRIS *(Now really serious, shaking his head.)* Better where you are.

MR WHITE I should like to see those old temples and holy men and jugglers . . . What was it you started telling me the other day about a monkey's paw or something, Morris?

MORRIS *(Hastily.)* Nothing. Leastways, nothing worth hearing.

MRS WHITE *(Curiously.)* Monkey's paw?

MORRIS *(Off-handedly.)* Well, it's just a bit of what you might call magic, perhaps.

(The three listeners lean forward eagerly. MORRIS absent-mindedly puts his empty glass to his lips and sets it down again. MR WHITE refills it once more, but all eyes are on MORRIS as he reaches into his jacket pocket and brings out the paw.)

To look at, it's just an ordinary little paw, dried to a mummy.

(He offers it to MRS WHITE, who draws back with a grimace, but HERBERT, fascinated by MORRIS's stories, accepts it eagerly and examines it curiously. MR WHITE takes it from his son, examining it in his turn and placing it carefully on the table.)

MR WHITE And what is there special about it?

MORRIS *(He pauses, weighing his words.)* It had a spell put on it by an old fakir, a very holy man. He wanted to show that fate

mummy *Something that was once living, now dried and preserved.*

fakir *(pronounced* fay-keer*) An Indian holy man.*

ruled people's lives, and that those who interfered with it, did so to their sorrow. He put a spell on it so that three separate men could each have three wishes from it.

(MR WHITE laughs, but MORRIS's manner is so impressive that the laughter jars somewhat.)

HERBERT Well, why don't you have three, sir?

MORRIS *(He looks at HERBERT and his face whitens.)* I have.

MRS WHITE And did you really have your three wishes granted?

(MORRIS raises the glass to his lips and it taps against his teeth as he drinks.)

MORRIS I did.

HERBERT *(Persistently.)* And has anybody else wished?

MORRIS The first man had his three wishes, yes. I don't know what the first two were, but the third, I suspect, was for death. That's how I got the paw.

(His tones are so grave that a hush falls upon the group.)

MR WHITE If you've had your three wishes, it's no good to you now then, Morris. What do you keep it for?

MORRIS *(Slowly.)* Difficult to explain. I did have some idea of selling it, but I don't think I will. It has caused enough mischief already. Besides, people won't buy. They think it's a fairy tale, some of them; and those who do think anything of it want to try it first and pay me afterwards.

MR WHITE *(Eyeing him keenly.)* If you could have another three wishes, would you have them?

MORRIS I don't know. I don't know.

(MORRIS takes the paw and, dangling it between thumb and forefinger, suddenly throws it onto the fire. MR WHITE shouts out, stoops down and snatches it off.)

Better let it burn

MR WHITE If you don't want it, Morris, give it to me.

MORRIS I won't. I threw it on the fire. If you keep it, don't blame me for what happens. Pitch it on the fire again, like a sensible man.

MR WHITE *(Shaking his head and examining his new possession.)* How do you do it?

MORRIS Hold it up in your right hand and wish aloud. But I warn you of the consequences.

MRS WHITE *(Getting up to put the kettle on.)* Sounds like *The Arabian Nights*. Don't you think you might wish for four pairs of hands for me?

(MR WHITE draws the paw out of his pocket, and all three burst out laughing as MORRIS, with a look of alarm on his face, catches hold of his arm. But they are quietened once more by the Sergeant-Major's tone.)

MORRIS *(Gruffly.)* If you must wish, wish for something sensible.

MRS WHITE *(Slightly awkwardly, covering the difficult moment.)* A cup of tea, Mr Morris?

MORRIS *(Rising.)* No. No, thank you. It's a long journey back and a

The Arabian Nights *Ancient tales (including those about Ali Baba, Aladdin and Sinbad) told by Arab story-tellers; also known as 'The Thousand and One Nights'.*

nasty night. Thank you for your hospitality, Mrs White. *(HERBERT helps him on with his coat, and MR WHITE opens the door for him.)* And remember what I said, White. Best to throw it on the fire.

(He looks at all three, nods, and leaves. There is a brief silence after his departure – he has put a dampener on the evening – but HERBERT breaks the spell, sitting down in the chair that MORRIS has just vacated.)

HERBERT If the tale about the monkey's paw is not more truthful than the others he has been telling us, we shan't get much out of it.

MR WHITE He seemed seriously insistent that I should throw it away.

HERBERT Very likely. *(Jokingly.)* We're going to be rich and famous and happy! Wish to be an emperor, father, to begin with – then you can't be hen-pecked!

(MRS WHITE throws a tea-towel at him and they both laugh, but her husband is eyeing the paw dubiously.)

MR WHITE I don't know what to wish for, and that's a fact. It seems to me I've got all I want.

HERBERT *(Putting his hand on his father's shoulder.)* If only you cleared the mortgage payments on the house, you'd be happy, wouldn't you? Well, wish for two hundred pounds, then: that'll just do it.

(MR WHITE stands up and, smiling in embarrassment at his own credulity, holds up the paw as his son, with a solemn face

hen-pecked *Nagged by his wife.*

dubiously *With some doubts in his mind.*

mortgage payments *Monthly payments to a building society or bank, repaying the loan taken out to buy the house.*

credulity *Willingness to believe unlikely things.*

[somewhat marred by a wink at his mother] sits down at the piano and strikes a few impressive and dramatic chords.)

MR WHITE *(Speaking very distinctly.)* I wish for two hundred pounds.

(HERBERT accompanies his father's words with a fine crash on the piano, but it is interrupted by a shuddering cry from the old man, who flings the paw to the floor, as his wife and son run to him.)

It moved! *(In disgust.)* As I wished, it twisted in my hand like a snake.

HERBERT *(Picking up the paw and replacing it on the table.)* Well, I don't see the money, and I bet I never shall.

MRS WHITE *(Regarding her husband anxiously.)* It must have been your imagination, father.

MR WHITE *(Shaking his head.)* Never mind, though; there's no harm done. But it gave me a shock all the same.

MRS WHITE *(Comfortingly.)* Come to bed. It's been a long evening. I expect you're tired.

(She goes up the stairs. HERBERT follows, but pauses at the top to add a parting shot.)

HERBERT I expect you'll find the cash tied up in a big bag in the middle of your bed . . . And something horrible squatting up on top of your wardrobe as you pocket your ill-gotten gains!

(He exits, chuckling to himself, and leaves the old man alone, sitting in his chair, gazing into the fire. Absent-mindedly he reaches for his drink on the table. Grasping the monkey's paw by mistake, he shudders, wipes his hand on his coat and, giving the paw a final uneasy glance, goes up to bed.)

(As he ascends the stairs, music fades up and the lights fade down to darkness.)

DISCUSSION: Discuss what you think they might have been talking about on page 31 to make the conversation turn serious.

DISCUSSION: A fakir, or holy man, is said to have put a spell on the paw 'to show that fate rules people's lives and that those who interfered with it, did so to their sorrow.' Discuss what 'fate' is.

ACTING: Act out the script from 'Thirty-one years of it . . . ' (line 66) to Morris's exit, bringing out the contrast between the White family's light-hearted attitude to the paw and Morris's reactions to it.

ACTING: Act out the end of Scene 2, from 'If only you cleared the mortgage . . . ' (line 168), showing exactly what happens when Mr White makes his wish and how he reacts after that.

WRITING: Write Herbert's diary entry for that night, in which he recounts Morris's visit and expresses his attitude to the paw and his father's wish.

Scene 3

When the lights come up again and the music fades, it is morning. A wintry sun is streaming in through the window, and MRS WHITE is clearing the mid-morning tea-cups, as MR WHITE, relaxed and cheerful now after the previous evening's unease, is smoking a pipe.

MRS WHITE I suppose all old soldiers are the same. The idea of our listening to such nonsense! How could wishes be granted in these days? And if they could, how could two hundred pounds hurt you, father? *(Laughing.)* Herbert said it might drop out of the sky on to your head!

MR WHITE Morris said the things happened so naturally that you might, if you so wished, attribute them to coincidence.

(There is a rattle and a letter drops through the letter-box. They look at each other and MRS WHITE goes to the mat and picks it up.)

Well?

MRS WHITE *(She takes out the letter and laughs.)* A gas bill!

(MR WHITE joins in the laugh at their expense.)

Herbert will have some more of his funny remarks, I expect, when he gets home from Meggins's.

MR WHITE I dare say. But, for all that, the thing moved in my hand; that I'll swear to.

MRS WHITE *(Soothingly.)* You thought it did.

attribute them to coincidence *You could claim that anything which happened as a result of a wish was, in fact, just a coincidence.*

MR WHITE I say it did. There was no 'thought' about it. I had just . . . What's the matter?

(He has noticed that his wife is staring out of the window.)

MRS WHITE A man, very well dressed. He seems to be unsure about coming in.

MR WHITE *(Cynically.)* A solicitor perhaps? Come to inform us that we have inherited two hundred pounds from a distant relative?

MRS WHITE He's coming down the path.

(She removes her apron, stuffs it behind a cushion and, answering the three knocks, opens the door on a nervous-looking stranger, ROBINSON.)

ROBINSON *(Clearly ill at ease.)* Mr and Mrs White?

MRS WHITE Yes, do come in, Mr . . . ?

ROBINSON Robinson. I . . . I was asked to call. *(He stoops and picks a thread of cotton from his trousers.)* I come from Meggins's Manufactory.

MRS WHITE *(Instantly frightened.)* Has anything happened to Herbert? What is it? What is it?

MR WHITE *(Interrupting hastily.)* There, there, mother. Sit down and don't jump to conclusions. You've not brought bad news, I'm sure, sir.

(Hoping for reassurance himself, MR WHITE eyes the visitor wistfully.)

ROBINSON I'm sorry . . .

MRS WHITE *(Wildly.)* Is he hurt?

cynically Sarcastically – refusing to believe in the romantic idea that they will ever receive the money he has wished for.

wistfully As though sadly wishing that something good might happen.

ROBINSON *(Quietly.)* Badly hurt. But he is not in any pain.

MRS WHITE Oh, thank God! Thank God for that! Thank . . .

(She breaks off suddenly as the sinister meaning of ROBINSON's assurance dawns upon her and she sees the awful confirmation of her fears in his averted face. She catches her breath and turns to her husband, laying her trembling old hand upon his. There is a long silence.)

ROBINSON *(In a low voice.)* He was caught in the machinery.

MR WHITE *(Dazed.)* Caught in the machinery . . . Yes.

(He sits staring blankly out of the window, still holding his wife's hand, and then turns gently to the visitor.)

He was the only one left to us. It is hard.

(ROBINSON coughs, walks slowly to the window and speaks without turning round.)

ROBINSON The firm wished me to convey their sincere sympathy with you in your great loss. I beg that you will understand I am only their servant and merely obeying orders.

(There is no reply. The old woman's face is white and on the old man's face is a look such as his friend the Sergeant-Major might have carried into his first action.)

I wish to say that Meggins disclaim all responsibility. They admit no liability at all. But, in consideration of your son's services, they wish to present you with a certain sum in compensation.

averted *Turned away.*

disclaim all responsibility . . . admit no liability . . . *The company refuse to accept that the accident was in any way their fault.*

in compensation *To make up for their loss.*

(MR WHITE drops his wife's hand and gazes with a look of horror at ROBINSON.)

MR WHITE *(Managing to shape with his lips the words.)* How much?

ROBINSON Two hundred pounds.

(Unaware of his wife's shriek, the old man smiles faintly, puts out his hand like a sightless man and drops, senseless, to the floor.)

(Blackout and sudden, jarring music.)

FREEZE-FRAMING AND ACTING: Freeze-frame the moment when the Whites realise that they are to receive £200; then act out the end of the scene, from Robinson's arrival, bringing out his awkwardness and the Whites' changing reactions.

DISCUSSION AND WRITING: There is only one scene to go. Predict the possible endings and discuss why they might be suitable.

SCENE 4

It is late evening ten days later. MRS WHITE sits staring into space as her husband silently finishes washing up their supper things. A church clock is heard striking ten.

MR WHITE *(Gently.)* Come to bed now. The fire's died down; you'll get cold.

MRS WHITE It is colder for my son.

(And she begins to weep afresh, as her husband winds the clock and goes up to bed. But before he is half way up the stairs, he is stopped by a sudden wild cry from his wife.)

The paw! The monkey's paw!

MR WHITE *(Descending the stairs, alarmed.)* Where? Where is it? What's the matter?

(She stumbles across the room and grabs him.)

MRS WHITE *(Quietly.)* I want the paw. You've not destroyed it?

MR WHITE *(Bewildered by her behaviour.)* It's on the mantel-piece in the tea-tin. Why?

MRS WHITE *(Laughing hysterically and crying at the same time.)* I only just thought of it. Why didn't I think of it before? Why didn't you think of it?

MR WHITE Think of what?

MRS WHITE *(Urgently.)* The other two wishes. We've only had one.

MR WHITE *(Fiercely.)* Wasn't that enough?

hysterically *In extreme uncontrolled excitement.*

MRS WHITE *(Triumphantly.)* No! We'll have one more. Go and get it and wish our boy alive again!

MR WHITE *(Aghast.)* Good God, you're mad!

MRS WHITE Get it. Get it quickly and wish – Oh, my boy, my boy!

MR WHITE *(Unsteadily.)* Go to bed. You don't know what you're saying.

MRS WHITE We had the first wish granted – why not the second?

MR WHITE A coincidence.

MRS WHITE *(Quivering with excitement.)* Go and get it and wish.

MR WHITE *(He looks at her steadily, his voice shaking.)* He has been dead ten days. And besides, he – I wouldn't tell you else, but – I could only recognise him by his clothing. If he was too terrible for you to see then, how now?

MRS WHITE *(Snatching the tin from the mantel-piece and thrusting it into his hands.)* Bring him back! Do you think I fear the child I have nursed?

(There is no opposing her. His brow cold with sweat, he pulls the lid off the tin and takes out the paw, his wife watching every move with upturned expectant face.)

Wish!

MR WHITE *(Faltering.)* It is foolish and wicked.

MRS WHITE Wish!

(Holding the paw aloft, he does as she demands.)

MR WHITE I wish my son alive again.

(The paw falls to the floor and he regards it fearfully, then sinks trembling into his chair as the old woman, with burning eyes, stumbles to the window and opens the curtains.)

(For some time they remain like this and then we hear the church clock chiming the quarter. With an unspeakable sense of relief at the failure of the paw, the old man rises and ascends the

stairs to the bedroom. His wife remains for a few moments, gazing with decreasing hope out of the window. Then she too slowly climbs the stairs and the room is empty.)

(So quiet as to be scarcely audible, there is a knock on the front door.)

MRS WHITE *(Off stage, from upstairs.)* What was that?

MR WHITE *(Unsteadily.)* A rat . . . a rat . . . it passed me on the stairs.

(This time unmistakably, a louder knock resounds through the house. MRS WHITE appears at the top of the stairs.)

MRS WHITE *(Screaming.)* It's Herbert! It's Herbert!

(Before she can descend, MR WHITE grabs at her arm.)

MR WHITE *(Whispering hoarsely.)* What are you going to do?

MRS WHITE It's my boy! It's Herbert! I forgot, the graveyard is a mile away. What are you holding me for? Let go. I must open the door!

MR WHITE For God's sake, don't let it in!

MRS WHITE *(Struggling to get free.)* You're afraid of your own son. Let me go. I'm coming, Herbert, I'm coming.

(There is another knock, and another, and the old woman, with a sudden wrench, breaks free and runs down the stairs. Watching in horror, MR WHITE sees his wife rattling back the chain and drawing the bottom bolt stiffly out of its socket. He sees her turn the key, and, only when she stretches up to undo the top bolt, is he galvanised into action.)

The bolt! Help me! I can't reach it!

with decreasing hope *Her hope that her son will return is steadily fading.*

scarcely audible *The sound can hardly be heard.*

galvanised into action *Shocked into doing something.*

(But her husband is on his hands and knees, groping in the semi-darkness for the paw. A torrent of knocks echoes through the house as the old woman drags a chair to the door, stands on it and grips the one bolt keeping the door securely shut. Straining every muscle, she forces the bolt down and, as she almost falls from the chair in her haste to open the door and greet whatever waits outside, her husband finds the paw and frantically breathes his third and final wish.)

(The knocking ceases suddenly, although the echoes still resound through the house. As the door is flung open, a cold wind rushes up the staircase and a long wail of disappointment and misery from his wife gives the old man the courage to run to her side and then out of the door to the gate beyond. As she collapses, weeping, the door swings fully open to reveal a silent and deserted road.)

(Gradually, as the lights dim, we hear the sounds of the Indian forest.)

ACTING: There are a large number of brief stage directions in this final scene (mainly consisting of single verbs or adverbial phrases). Act out the beginning of the scene (up to 'Wish!'), paying particular attention to the stage directions and discuss the very different emotions displayed by Mr White and Mrs White. Then think up alternative stage directions which you think would work and discuss the effect that they would have on the interpretation of the characters.

DISCUSSION: What exactly is Mr White's final wish? Suggest exactly which words you think he might say and discuss why he would choose them.

DISCUSSION: Discuss exactly what you think has happened at the end of the play and what effect it has when we hear the sounds of the Indian forest once again.

DISCUSSION: 'Morris said the things happened so naturally that you might, if you wished, attribute them to coincidence.' Discuss whether, in your opinion, all the events could be attributed to coincidence or whether the story suggests that the paw is responsible for what happens.

Dramascripts

The Canterville Ghost

OSCAR WILDE

Adapted by

John O'Connor

OSCAR WILDE

Born in Dublin in 1854, the son of a famous surgeon father and successful writer mother, Oscar Fingal O'Flahertie Wills Wilde proved to be a brilliant scholar and by his late twenties, was already dazzling London society with his wit and much-quoted conversation. He is now mainly known for his plays, especially *The Importance of Being Earnest*, generally regarded as a comic masterpiece, but also wrote a great deal of poetry, many short stories and several novels, including the mysterious and macabre *Picture of Dorian Grey* in 1890. At the height of his theatrical success in 1895, Wilde was imprisoned for homosexuality – it was then an offence – and, on his release three years later, went to live in France, where he wrote 'The Ballad of Reading Gaol', inspired by his prison experience. He died in Paris in 1900, aged only 46.

The Scenes

Scene 1	The hall, Canterville Chase
Scene 2	The library
Scene 3	The hall, midnight
Scene 4	The bedroom landing, the next night
Scene 5	A corridor, the next night
Scene 6	A corridor, a week later
Scene 7	The library, a month later
Scene 8	The hall, later that day
Scene 9	The hall, later that day
Scene 10	The dungeon

Staging

A panelled Elizabethan room will serve for all scenes, if pieces of furniture or other decorations are changed to signify different locations in Canterville Chase. The dungeon effect in the final scene is best achieved with lighting, rather than the creation of a separate set.

It is worth taking trouble over making – or acquiring – realistic and interesting props and costumes. While the ghost does not need complete changes of costume for each haunting, it will be important to show that he has made an effort.

Music

Appropriately spooky music (especially between scenes) and realistic sound effects will add greatly to the impact.

THE CHARACTERS

LORD CANTERVILLE *present owner of Canterville Chase.*

MRS UMNEY *the ancient house-keeper.*

HIRAM B OTIS *the American ambassador and new tenant of Canterville Chase.*

MARTHA OTIS *his wife.*

WASHINGTON OTIS *their son; 20.*

VIRGINIA OTIS *their daughter; 15.*

'STARS' *and* **'STRIPES'** *their twin sons; 11.*

THE GHOST . . . *of Sir Simon Canterville; died 1584.*

Lord Canterville and the ghost should have very 'plummy' English accents; the Otises can come from any part of America, but the parents will have stronger accents than the children (who are beginning to be influenced by their stay in England).

The Canterville Ghost

Scene 1

The hall of Canterville Chase, near Ascot, Berkshire, November 1 1884. Servants puffing under the weight of numerous chests, trunks, boxes, tennis rackets and fishing rods, tell us that people are moving in.

Enter from left an English aristocrat, LORD CANTERVILLE, and the new tenant, HIRAM B OTIS, the latter smoking a cheroot. They are followed at a respectful distance by the ancient housekeeper, MRS UMNEY.

LORD CANTERVILLE . . . And, as I pointed out to you, Mr Otis, when we met to discuss the terms of the lease, Canterville Chase is undoubtedly haunted. We have not cared to live in the place ourselves since my grand-aunt, the Duchess of Bolton, was frightened into a fit, from which she never really recovered, by two skeleton hands being placed on her shoulders as she was dressing for dinner. And I feel bound to tell you, Mr Otis, that the ghost has been seen by several living members of my family, as well as by the rector of the parish, the Reverend Augustus Dampier. After the unfortunate accident to the Duchess, none of the younger servants would stay with us, and Lady Canterville often got very little sleep at night in consequence of the mysterious noises that came from the corridor and the library.

HIRAM My lord, I will include the ghost in with the furniture as part of the deal. I come from a modern country, where we have everything that money can buy, and I reckon that if

cheroot *Small cigar.*

terms of the lease *The details of the contract signed when they rented the house.*

there were such a thing as a ghost in Europe, we'd have it at home in a pretty short time in one of our museums.

LORD CANTERVILLE *(Smiling.)* I fear that the ghost exists. It has been well known for three centuries, since 1584 in fact, and always makes its appearance before the death of any member of our family.

HIRAM Well, so does the family doctor, for that matter, Lord Canterville. But there is no such thing, sir, as a ghost, and I guess the laws of nature are not going to be suspended for the British aristocracy.

(During HIRAM's speech, a carriage has been heard pulling up outside, followed by the excited chatter of the rest of the Otis family. LORD CANTERVILLE has had enough of this sceptical

sceptical *Hiram does not accept superstitious beliefs.*

American and takes this as an excuse to take his leave.)

LORD CANTERVILLE I will ask Mrs Umney to give you a tour of the house. She has been house-keeper here for over forty years and will have her own stories to tell. If there is anything you need. . .

(He bows stiffly and exits just as the family enter, left. The twins 'STARS' and 'STRIPES' run in first, firing pea-shooters at each other, almost knocking over the departing lord, rush across the stage and exit through the other door. MRS MARTHA OTIS follows with her other children, WASHINGTON and VIRGINIA, and greets MRS UMNEY warmly.)

MARTHA You must be Mrs Umney. Lord Canterville has told us all about you.

MRS UMNEY *(Reserved: she doesn't know quite what to make of these Americans.)* How do you do, madam. I bid you welcome to Canterville Chase. Tea is laid out in the library.

MARTHA Thank you. We'll follow.

(VIRGINIA and WASHINGTON exchange mischievous glances as their mother exits after MRS UMNEY, through the door, right. HIRAM continues to admire the portraits for a second, still puffing on his cheroot, and then wanders off in search of tea.)

Scene 2

The library. The family, now armed with cups of tea and platefuls of cake, enter left, followed by MRS UMNEY. Immediately MARTHA notices something on the carpet.

MARTHA Mrs Umney, I'm afraid something appears to have been spilt on the floor.

MRS UMNEY *(In a low, sepulchral voice.)* Yes, madam. Blood has been spilt on that spot.

MARTHA How horrid! I don't at all care for blood-stains in a sitting room. It must be removed at once.

MRS UMNEY *(Smiling knowingly, but in the same low, mysterious voice.)* It is the blood of Lady Eleanore de Canterville, madam, who was murdered on that very spot by her own husband, Sir Simon de Canterville, in 1575. Sir Simon survived her by nine years, and disappeared suddenly under very mysterious circumstances. His body has never been discovered, but his guilty spirit still haunts the Chase. The blood-stain has been much admired by tourists and others, and cannot be removed.

WASHINGTON Nonsense! Pinkerton's Champion Stain Remover and Paragon Detergent will clean it up in no time!

(And before the appalled housekeeper can interfere, WASHINGTON has fallen to his knees and is scouring the stain with the contents of a small bottle and cloth produced from his pocket. After only a couple of seconds, he leaps to his feet triumphantly.)

sepulchral *Dramatically gloomy; to do with death and the grave.*

There! I knew Pinkerton would do it!

(The congratulations of his admiring family are cut short by a terrible flash of lightning and a fearful peal of thunder, all of which is too much for MRS UMNEY, who promptly faints.)

HIRAM *(Ignoring MRS UMNEY and calmly lighting another cheroot.)* What a monstrous climate! I guess the old country is so over-populated that they don't have enough decent weather for everybody.

MARTHA *(Looking down at the prostrate housekeeper.)* My dear Hiram, what can we do with a woman who faints?

HIRAM Charge it to her, like breakages: she won't faint after that. *(Noticing VIRGINIA, who is studying something on the window-pane.)* What's caught your eye, Virginia?

VIRGINIA Somebody seems to have scratched a message on the glass. *(She struggles to read out the ancient writing.)*

'When a golden girl can win
Prayer from out the lips of sin,
When the barren almond bears,

Charge it to her, like breakages *Servants had money deducted from their wages whenever they broke anything; Hiram suggests that this should happen to Mrs Umney every time she faints.*

> And a little child gives away its tears,
> Then shall all the house be still
> And peace come to Canterville.'

It's some kind of prophecy.

HIRAM Looks like a job for Watson's Window Wash. *(Turns to MARTHA.)* Come, my dears, shall we continue our tour of the house?

(The family exit, right, leaving MRS UMNEY on the floor. Realising that they have gone, she sits up with a jerk, scrambles to her feet and follows them, pausing only to skirt round the clean patch on the carpet.)

MRS UMNEY *(Muttering to herself.)* As God is my witness, no good will come of it . . .

(Accompanied by appropriately spooky music, the lights fade to blackout.)

IMPROVISATION: Improvise a conversation between Mrs Umney and Lord Canterville, in which she describes what happened in Scene 2 and predicts what will 'come of it', while he reacts appropriately. Exaggerate the characters for comic effect.

WRITING: Write a blurb for a leaflet advertising visits to Canterville Chase, which includes a reference to the ghost as an attractive feature and gives details of the sixteenth century murder and its aftermath.

DISCUSSION: Discuss what you think the meaning might be of the rhyme scratched on the window. (Clearly it will have some connection to the story of the ghost and the Otis family.)

SCENE 3

In the hall, a clock chimes midnight and the lights fade up on HIRAM, who has clearly fallen asleep in an armchair, book in hand, after a little too much wine, and is snoring loudly. He is awoken by a curious noise, off stage: a clank of metal getting louder, and now accompanied by footsteps. As he gets to his feet, the apparition enters. It is an old man of terrible aspect. His eyes are red-rimmed like burning coals; long grey hair falls over his shoulders in matted coils; his garments, of antique cut, are soiled and ragged; and from his wrists and ankles hang heavy manacles and rusty chains. HIRAM is appalled . . .

HIRAM My dear sir, I really must insist on your oiling those chains, and *(Reaching into his dressing-gown pocket.)* have brought you for that purpose a small bottle of the Tammany Rising Sun Lubricator. It is said to be completely efficacious upon one application, and there are several testimonials to that effect on the wrapper. I shall leave it here for you by the armchair and will be happy to supply you with more, should you require it.

(With these words, HIRAM collects his book and goes off to bed. For a moment the GHOST of Sir Simon de Canterville stands motionless in silent indignation. He can hardly believe this, and he slumps in the armchair, completely bewildered.)

of terrible aspect *The ghost looks extremely frightening.*

of antique cut *Extremely old-fashioned in design.*

efficacious *Effective; a word often used in nineteenth-century advertisements for cleaning fluids.*

testimonials *Written statements supporting the effectiveness of the product.*

in silent indignation *He cannot find words to express his anger.*

GHOST First the blood-stain and now this! Never in a brilliant and uninterrupted career of three hundred years, have I been so grossly insulted! Think of the Duchess, frightened into a fit as she stood by her glass in her lace and diamonds; the four housemaids who went off in hysterics when I merely grinned at them through the curtains; the butler who shot himself in the pantry because he saw a green hand tapping at the window pane. Think of my celebrated appearance as 'Gaunt Gibeon, the Blood-sucker of Bexley Moor'; and the terror I caused by playing skittles with my own bones on the tennis-court!

And, after all this, some wretched modern Americans come here and offer me the Rising Sun Lubricator! It is quite intolerable! No ghost in history has ever been treated in this manner. *(Leaping to his feet.)* I have it! The demonic laughter! This cannot fail – was it not said to have turned Lord Raker's wig grey in a single night?

(Taking a deep breath, he accordingly laughs his most horrible laugh, till the vaulted roof rings and rings. But there is no reaction. Try again, he thinks, but no sooner has he taken a deep breath for the second time, than MARTHA enters. Standing in the doorway, she is an impressive sight in her dressing-gown and curlers.)

MARTHA *(Severely.)* It is clear that you are far from well. I have therefore brought you down a bottle of Dr Dobell's Tincture. If it is indigestion, you will find it a most excellent remedy.

(The GHOST glares at her in fury, but his plans to turn himself into a monstrous black dog are thwarted by her exit and he can do nothing but curse his failure.)

hysterics *Uncontrolled panic attacks.*

Tincture *Medicine based upon alcohol.*

GHOST This calls for some serious haunting! I will be revenged . . . tomorrow! *(He strides off towards the door and then turns.)* Or my name is not Sir Simon Canterville!

(As he storms out, there is a peal of thunder and a blackout.)

Scene 4

The bedroom landing, the next night. The clock strikes midnight and the GHOST enters, holding a parchment in one hand and ticking off items on his schedule with a quill pen in the other.

GHOST First I make my way to Washington Otis's room, gibber at him from the foot of the bed and stab myself three times in the throat to the sound of sad music. I hold him responsible for constantly removing the famous Canterville blood-stain each time it is replaced, by means of Pinkerton's Paragon Detergent.

Having reduced this reckless and foolhardy youth to a condition of abject terror, I will then proceed to the room occupied by the Ambassador and his wife, there to place a clammy hand upon Mrs Otis's forehead while hissing into her trembling husband's ear the secrets of the charnel-house.

With regard to Virginia, she has not insulted me in any particular way, and a few hollow groans from the wardobe will suffice. I am determined, however, to teach the twins a lesson. I shall stand between their beds in the form of a green, icy-cold corpse, till they become paralysed with fear, then throw off the winding-sheet and crawl round the room, with white bleached bones and one rolling eyeball, in the character of 'Dumb Daniel, or the Suicide's Skeleton'. *(He ticks off the final item, stuffs the parchment and pen into*

abject *Utterly miserable.*

charnel-house *Building where the bones of the dead were stored.*

winding-sheet *Cloth in which corpses were wrapped.*

his doublet, and stands to attention determinedly, chuckling to himself.) Now for revenge!

(As he turns to commence his haunting, however, he is stopped in his tracks and recoils in a piteous wail of terror; for there, barring his way and illuminated only by a shaft of moonlight shining through the curtains, is a terrifying spectre. Motionless as a carven image and monstrous as a madman's dream, its head is bald and shiny; its face round and fat; and hideous laughter seems to have writhed its features into an eternal grin. A foul garment, like his own, swathes its ghastly form, an ancient sword hangs from a withered arm, and on its breast is a placard bearing strange writing.)

(Never having seen another ghost before, the GHOST turns to flee, but, in his desperation to escape he trips over the curtains, which flap apart. This has two effects. The first is that more moonlight floods the corridor; the second is that, in the ensuing draught, the visiting 'spectre' topples to the floor. Picking himself up, the GHOST of Sir Simon cautiously approaches . . . And finds, now heaped in a disordered pile, a white curtain, a broom, a kitchen knife and a hollow turnip. On the piece of paper pinned to the sheet are the following words, which he reads out:

'YE OTIS GHOST,
Ye Onlie True & Original Spook
Beware of Ye Imitations
All others are Counterfeit'

Furious at the insult and the trickery played upon him, he grinds his toothless gums together and, holding his hand aloft, swears a solemn oath.)

Deeds of blood will be wrought and Murder will walk abroad with silent feet!

(And he storms off, still muttering to himself.)

ARTWORK: Draw the twins' 'ghost' and, if possible, make a version of it to be used in a production of the play.

ARTWORK: Imagine that you are making a film version of The Canterville Ghost. Storyboard Scene 4 in five or six frames, bringing out the visually comic effects. (For an example of storyboarding, see page 6.)

Scene 5

The next night. 'STARS' and 'STRIPES' enter in pyjamas. They tie a wire across the corridor and exit, giggling. Enter from the opposite door, the GHOST, looking determined but less confident than before.

GHOST Enter 'Black Isaac, or the Huntsman of Hodley Woods'! *(He creeps along the corridor.)* With some additional effects in the shape of monstrous baying hounds, this should frighten the little horrors out of their wi . . .

(But he does not complete his sentence. Meeting the trip-wire, he hurtles head-long off stage and his fall down the stairs is signalled by a prolonged crashing sound, ending in a pathetic whimper.)

(The twins enter from the direction of his fall and run across the stage, convulsed in laughter.)

SCENE 6

A week later. The clock strikes midnight and the GHOST enters, furtively. He is dressed in his traditional armour and makes a grating sound as he traverses the corridor, from left to right, and exits, looking over his shoulder to check that his movements have not been detected.

GHOST *(Off stage, accompanied by noises of rummaging through a* 1
kitchen cupboard.) Ah! *(Muffled.)*

(The GHOST re-enters, clutching a small container with a nozzle. It is a tin of Rising Sun Lubricator, and the ghost carefully – and extremely shamefacedly – oils the offending chains, and for good measure, the joints of his armour, before skulking off [now much more quietly] back to his coffin.)

traverses *Crosses.*

Scene 7

Mid-afternoon, a month later. HIRAM is at his desk in the library, composing a letter. Completing the final sentence, he sits back and reads it through.

HIRAM 'Canterville Chase, December first.

My dear Lord Canterville,

We have now been here exactly one month and this is just to report that the house is as comfortable as we could wish and that, after a few initial upsets, Mrs Umney has proved an excellent housekeeper. It looks as though we shall now be staying on at least until next spring.

By the way, you will be pleased to hear that the Canterville Ghost troubles us no longer.

Regards,

(Writing his signature with a flourish.) Hiram B. Otis.'

(As he smiles in satisfaction, folds the letter and places it in an envelope, the lights fade, to the accompaniment of sombre music.)

sombre *Serious and heavy.*

WRITING: Imagine that Lord Canterville writes back to Hiram, asking for further details of what has happened to the ghost and why he troubles them no longer. Write Hiram's reply, providing details based upon Scenes 2 to 6, and adding any other plausible stories of the family's treatment of the ghost.

SCENE 8

The hall, later that day. The GHOST sits in the window-seat, gazing out, his head leaning on his hand, his whole attitude one of extreme depression. He sighs heavily, and is so taken up by his own thoughts, that he at first fails to notice that VIRGINIA has entered and is watching him. She coughs quietly and the GHOST jumps.

VIRGINIA I'm sorry; I didn't mean to startle you.

GHOST It's not your fault. My nerves are so shattered these days, I start at the slightest noise.

VIRGINIA You seemed to be deep in thought.

GHOST Yes. I had just made up my mind to give up on the blood-stain on the library floor. I take the view that, if your family do not want it, they don't deserve it. But a ghost has responsibilities and I do not intend to give them up lightly.

VIRGINIA Responsibilities?

GHOST Yes. For example, it is my solemn duty to appear in the corridor once a week; and to gibber from the large stained-glass window on the first and third Wednesday of each month; and I really do not see how I can honourably escape from my obligations.

VIRGINIA I see your difficulty.

GHOST But I am trying to be as accommodating as possible. I now remove my boots, tread as lightly as I can, and am careful to use Rising Sun Lubricator for oiling my chains.

VIRGINIA And we still torment you.

GHOST You most certainly do. Only last week, while dressed for the part of 'Reckless Rupert, or the Headless Earl' – an extremely difficult make-up, which took fully three hours – I suffered a severe fall through treading on a butter-slide which your twin brothers had constructed from the entrance of the Tapestry Chamber to the top of the oak staircase. The shock to the system was considerable.

VIRGINIA *(Trying not to laugh.)* I can imagine.

GHOST And the only consolation in the whole affair was that I had not brought my head with me. *(VIRGINIA splutters and he gives her a severe look.)* Had I done so, the consequences might have been very serious.

VIRGINIA Indeed.

GHOST But what is a ghost supposed to do? Presumably I must henceforth content myself, as a rule, with creeping about the passages in slippers, wearing a thick red muffler for fear of draughts, and carrying a small pistol to protect myself against your twin brothers!

VIRGINIA I am sorry for you. But my brothers are going back to school tomorrow, and then, if you behave yourself, no-one will annoy you.

GHOST It is absurd asking me to behave myself. Quite absurd. I must rattle my chains, and groan through keyholes, and walk about at night, if that is what you mean. It is my only reason for existing.

VIRGINIA *(Seeing that she must take a firmer line.)* It is no reason at all for existing, and you know you have been very wicked. Old Mrs Umney told us that you had killed your wife.

GHOST *(Petulantly.)* Yes, I quite admit it. But it was purely a family matter, and concerned no-one else.

VIRGINIA It is very wrong to kill anyone.

petulantly *Sulking and irritable.*

GHOST My wife was very plain, never had my ruffs properly starched, and knew nothing about cookery. However, it is no matter now, for it is all over, and I don't think it was very nice of her brothers to starve me to death, even if I did kill her.

VIRGINIA Starve you to death? Oh, Mr Ghost – I mean, Sir Simon – are you hungry? I have a sandwich in my pocket. Would you like it?

GHOST No, thank you. I never eat anything now. But it is very kind of you, all the same, and you are much nicer than the rest of your horrid, rude, dishonest family.

VIRGINIA *(Stamping her foot.)* Stop! It is you who are rude and horrid. And, as for dishonesty, who was it stole the paints out of my box to try to replace that ridiculous blood-stain in the library?

GHOST Well, really, what was I to do? It is very difficult to get real blood nowadays. And, as your brother started it all with his Paragon Detergent, I certainly saw no reason why I should not have your paints.

VIRGINIA *(Annoyed at his unrepentant attitude.)* Well, good evening! I will go and ask papa to get the twins an extra week's holiday.

GHOST Oh, please don't go, Miss Virginia. I am so lonely and so unhappy, and I really don't know what to do. I want to sleep and cannot.

VIRGINIA Oh, don't be ridiculous! You have merely to go to bed and blow out the candle. Even babies know how to sleep, and they're not very clever.

ruffs *Collars worn in Elizabethan times.*

GHOST *(Sadly.)* I have not slept for three hundred years. For three hundred years I have not slept and I am so tired.

(VIRGINIA's eyes open in wonder and she becomes quite grave. She comes towards him and, kneeling by his side, looks up into his old withered face.)

VIRGINIA *(Murmuring.)* Poor, poor ghost. Have you no place where you can sleep?

(At first he does not reply. Then, in a low, dreamy voice, he speaks.)

GHOST Far away beyond the pinewoods, there is a little garden. There the grass grows long and deep, there are great white stars of the hemlock flower, there the nightingale sings all night long. All night long he sings, and the cold, crystal moon looks down, and the yew-tree spreads out its giant arms over the sleepers.

(VIRGINIA's eyes grow dim with tears and she hides her face in her hands.)

VIRGINIA *(Whispering.)* You mean the Garden of Death.

GHOST Yes, Death. Death must be so beautiful. To lie in the soft, brown earth, with the grasses waving above one's head, and listen to silence. To have no yesterday, and no tomorrow. To forget time, to forgive life, to be at peace. *(He looks down at her, realising something.)* You can help me. You can open for me the portals of Death's house, for Love is always with you, and Love is stronger than Death is.

(VIRGINIA trembles as a cold shudder runs through her and for a few moments there is silence. When the GHOST speaks again, his voice sounds like the sighing of the wind.)

hemlock *A plant from which poison is extracted.*

portals *Gates.*

Have you ever read the prophecy on the library window?

VIRGINIA Oh, often. I know it quite well:
'When a golden girl can win
Prayer from out the lips of sin,
When the barren almond bears,
And a little child gives away its tears,
Then shall all the house be still
And peace come to Canterville.'
But I don't know what it means.

GHOST *(Sadly.)* It means that you must weep for me, for my sins, because I have no tears, and pray for me, for my soul, because I have no faith, and then, if you have always been sweet, and good, and gentle, the Angel of Death will have mercy upon me. You will see fearful shapes in darkness, and wicked voices will whisper in your ear. But they will not harm you, for against your purity the powers of hell cannot prevail.

(Initially VIRGINIA makes no answer, and the GHOST wrings his hands in despair as he looks down at her bowed golden head. Suddenly she stands up, very pale, and with a strange light in her eyes.)

VIRGINIA *(Firmly.)* I am not afraid. And I will ask the Angel to have mercy upon you.

(The lights dim to blackout.)

WRITING OR ARTWORK: Re-read the ghost's description of the Garden of Death on page 69 (from 'Far away beyond the pinewoods . . .' to ' . . . to be at peace.' and either turn it into a poem, or draw a picture (or create a collage) which illustrates it.

WRITING: Write Virginia's diary entry in which she describes having met the ghost, discusses what his wishes are and thinks through what she must now do, as she is the only one who can help.

SCENE 9

The hall, later the same day. It is approaching midnight and there is general panic in the Otis household, as VIRGINIA has not been seen for some time. HIRAM is sending off messages, MARTHA is becoming increasingly hysterical and MRS UMNEY is reacting with tragic gloom.

MARTHA Oh, my poor Virginia!

HIRAM *(Chewing ferociously on an unlit cheroot.)* I have dispatched telegrams to every police inspector in the county, telling them to look out for a girl who might have been kidnapped to be held to ransom.

MRS UMNEY I said no good would come of it.

(Washington runs in.)

WASHINGTON *(Breathlessly.)* The station-master has no recollection of anyone answering Virginia's description, but a watch is being kept down the line.

MRS UMNEY *(Lugubriously.)* Has the carp-pond been dragged? *(MARTHA goes off into further hysterics.)*

WASHINGTON *(Acidly, glaring at the housekeeper.)* Yes. Without result, thank goodness.

(The clock in the tower starts to boom twelve.)

HIRAM Well, nothing more can be done tonight. I'll telegraph Scotland Yard again in the morning. I suggest the rest of you get some sleep; I'll wait up in case there's news.

lugubriously *Wallowing in gloom.*

(As the last stroke of twelve sounds, there is a terrific crash and a sudden shrill cry; a dreadful peal of thunder shakes the house, a strain of unearthly music floats through the air; a panel in the wall crashes outwards and – looking very pale and shaken, with a little box in her hand – in steps VIRGINIA. In a moment of indescribable relief, they all rush up to her and her mother clasps her in her arms.)

HIRAM *(Now angry.)* Good heavens, child! Where have you been? I've been riding all over the country looking for you, and your mother has been frightened to death. You must stop playing these practical jokes.

'STARS' / 'STRIPES' Except on the ghost! Except on the ghost!

MARTHA *(Kissing the trembling girl and smoothing the tangled gold of her hair.)* Thank God you are found!

VIRGINIA *(Quietly.)* Mama, Papa, I have been with the ghost. He is dead, and you must come and see him. He had been very wicked, but he was really sorry for all that he had done, and he gave me this box of beautiful jewels before he died.

(The whole family gaze at her in mute astonishment. Then, gravely and silently, she turns round and leads them through the opening in the panelling, as the lights dim to blackout.)

FREEZE-FRAMING AND ACTING: Freeze-frame the moment just after Virginia's appearance from behind the panel in the wall. Then act out the whole of Scene 9, showing the contrast between the frenetic opening and the calm ending.

DISCUSSION AND WRITING: Imagine that you are in charge of the sound effects and recorded music for a stage production of The Canterville Ghost. Discuss ideas for appropriate sound effects and music at selected moments in the play, and then draft a table showing which sound is used where.

Scene 10

A shaft of moonlight, coming from a small window high in the wall, illuminates centre-stage and in the gloom we can just make out that this is a dungeon. Embedded in the wall is a huge iron ring, and chained to it is a skeleton, stretched out full length on the floor and seeming to grasp with its long fleshless fingers an old-fashioned trencher and ewer, which appear to have been placed just out of reach.

Sounds are heard and the light from HIRAM's lantern shines in on the gloom, as the family enter in unaccustomed silence. They look in wonder at the terrible tragedy whose secret is at last disclosed to them.

Suddenly one of the twins, who has clambered up to look out of the window, cries out.

'STARS' Hello! The old withered almond tree has blossomed. I can see the flowers quite plainly in the moonlight. 1

(Virginia walks to the window and looks out.)

VIRGINIA He has been forgiven.

(The lights fade on the family, gathered around the last remains of Sir Simon Canterville, now at rest.)

ARTWORK: Draw the moment at which the family find the skeleton in the dungeon, following the description in the stage directions to Scene 10.

Looking Back at the Plays

1 Discussion: casting the roles

In pairs, pick one of the plays and discuss which film or television actors you would cast in each of the roles, noting down brief reasons to support your choices. Compare your ideas in a class discussion.

2 Artwork and writing: designing a poster

Work in pairs to design a poster advertising a stage, television or film version of one of the plays. First discuss as a class the words and images that usually appear on a poster of this kind.

3 Artwork and writing: a theatre programme

Create a programme for a theatre performance, either for one of the plays, or for a production in which all three would be put on together (a 'triple bill'). Remember to include a cast that you have decided on, as well as any illustrations that would be helpful to the audience.

4 Discussion and writing: a review

Which of the three plays did you enjoy most?

For each play, discuss features such as the plots, the characters, the dialogue, the setting and the level of excitement or mystery. Then write a review of the play you considered to be the best.

5 Writing: a supernatural thriller

Write a story of the supernatural which includes one of these:

- a spectre which seems to be predicting some awful happening
- events which seem to be dictated by fate
- a ghost who suffers at the hands of mortals.

6 Writing and improvisation

Imagine that an estate agent has the job of selling either the signal-box (converted into a small dwelling), the Whites' house in Laburnam Villas, or Canterville Chase. In pairs, write the details which would be sent out to potential buyers (e.g. 'A small signal-box, tastefully converted . . .'). Then improvise the situation, with one person being the potential buyer, asking questions about the features of the house ('What happened to the last people who lived here . . . ?' 'There seems to be something scratched on the window-pane . . . '), and the estate agent trying to find interesting but truthful explanations.

7 Discussion and writing: ten years on

Discuss what each of the following might be doing ten years after the ends of their stories: the Visitor (in The Signal-Man); Mrs White (in The Monkey's Paw); Virginia (in The Canterville Ghost). Then write a letter from the character to a friend, explaining how the events of ten years earlier have affected them.

8 Adapting from short story to play

In pairs, read the extract from the original short-story version of The Canterville Ghost. Discuss what the playwright has done in adapting the scene for the stage – it can be found on pages 65–67. These questions will help you.

- How much of the original dialogue has been used?
- What has been added and why?
- What are the strengths of the two different versions?

After this he was not seen again on any nocturnal expedition. The twins lay in wait for him on several occasions, and strewed the passages with nutshells every night to the great annoyance of their parents and the servants. But it was of no avail. It was generally assumed that the ghost had gone away, and, in fact, Mr Otis wrote a letter to that effect to Lord Canterville, who, in reply, expressed his great pleasure at the news, and sent his best congratulations to the Ambassador's worthy wife.

But one day a few weeks later, Virginia was going past the Tapestry Chamber when she fancied she saw someone inside. To her immense surprise, it was the Canterville ghost himself! He was sitting by the window, watching the ruined gold of the yellow trees fly through the air, and the red leaves dancing madly down the long avenue. His head was leaning on his hand, and his whole attitude was one of extreme depression. Indeed, so forlorn, and so much out of repair did he look, that Virginia, whose first idea had been to run away and lock herself in her room, was filled with pity, and determined to try and comfort him. So light was her footfall, and so deep his melancholy, that he was not aware of her presence till she spoke to him.

'I am so sorry for you,' she said, 'but my brothers are going back to school tomorrow, and then, if you behave yourself, no one will annoy you.'

'It is absurd asking me to behave myself,' he answered, looking round in astonishment at the pretty girl who had ventured to address him, 'quite absurd. I must rattle my chains, and groan through keyholes, and walk about at night, if that is what you mean. It is my only reason for existing.'

'It is no reason at all for existing, and you know you have been very wicked. Mrs Umney told us, the first day we arrived here, that you had killed your wife.'

'Well, I quite admit it,' said the ghost petulantly, 'but it was purely a family matter, and concerned no one else.'

'It is very wrong to kill anyone,' said Virginia.

9 Adapting from short story to play: the theme of fate

Two of the plays – The Signal-Man and The Monkey's Paw – are about Fate, and seem to suggest that there is no way in which it can be avoided. This is another story on the same theme. Read it carefully and then adapt a section of it for the stage, using some of the techniques that you have learned about from the three plays. Think about:

- the ways in which dialogue can be used to help tell the story
- the use of stage directions to help the reader understand what is going on when there is no dialogue
- especially how the figure of Death might be presented in a stage performance.

The Lord, The Steward and the Visit of Death

Many centuries ago, in a castle just a day's ride from the ancient city of Baghdad, lived a great lord. Though rich and powerful, his people loved him, for he treated servants well, fed his followers upon the best foods, and was fair and just in his dealings. Among the members of his household was a young steward, whose task it was to visit the market-place each day and buy fresh produce: fruits, meat and hot bread from the many tradespeople who depended for their livelihood on the lord and his household.

Leaving the castle gates at dawn one morning, this steward made his way down the sandy road to the market, as he had been in the habit of doing since inheriting the title of steward from his now ageing father. He approached the town and heard the familiar sounds of the market traders, saw the familiar stalls and smelled the familiar smells. But, as he entered the market-place, something was not quite right. The sights, sounds and smells were not exactly as they usually were. There was a strange, unsettling feeling in the air, something that he could not put his finger on, but which disturbed his peace of mind, made him look over his shoulder at every turn, examine every familiar face to see whether the market-people had felt the strangeness too.

It was then, pushing through the crowded street, that he saw it. Huddled in a shadowed doorway, a grey cloak shrouding its face, was a figure. There were many beggars in the market, but this was not a beggar – there was no outstretched hand or cry for alms. Instead, the figure simply stood there, as though waiting. And the steward knew, with an unshakeable conviction, that it was waiting for him, and that he had to approach it.

Each small step towards the dark doorway seemed to take an hour, and the street, though thronging with a great press of people, seemed empty but for him and the waiting figure. At last he reached it and, stretching out his hand to touch his terrifying companion on the shoulder, its cloak slipped back, and the steward saw what he had known from the first moment, that this was indeed Death, and that Death had come for him.

How he managed to struggle back to the castle, overwhelmed with terror and loathing as he was, he could not say. But arrive he did, and he was shown into the great chamber, where his master was waiting for him.

'I have heard of your terror,' said the lord anxiously, and the steward told him all that had happened, how he had seen the figure of Death himself in the market-place, and how he knew for certain that it had come for him, that it was his time.

The lord thought for a moment and then, grasping his steward's hand, said, 'You have nothing to fear. Take this gold, take my finest, fastest white stallion from the stable, fly from this place, journey for a day and hide yourself in the streets of Baghdad. No-one will find you there. I myself will go down to the market-place and banish Death. When he is gone, you may return and live out your days in peace and contentment.'

Overjoyed at his master's kindness, the young steward fled from the castle, rode like the wind for a day and, as the lord had directed, hid himself in the darkest street of busy Baghdad.

The lord, meanwhile, left the castle, as his steward had done earlier that day, strode determinedly down to the town and entered the market-place. He knew – how he could not have said – where to find Death and, unafraid, he approached him, still crouched in his darkened doorway. Boldly the lord snatched the cowl from off the figure's head and challenged him, as though addressing some invading baron or robber-knight: 'I know who you are and why you appear. But why do you terrify my steward? He is young – you can surely have no dealings with him?'

Death looked at the lord, a strange, questioning look. There was nothing defiant in it, nothing to suggest the power that Death truly held. And when he spoke, it was in a tone that the lord afterwards described as puzzled.

'I am truly sorry that I frightened your steward,' said Death. 'It was just that I was surprised.'

'Surprised? Surprised at what?' asked the lord.

'Surprised to see him here,' replied Death. And suddenly fixing the lord with the coldest of looks, he added, 'You see, I have an appointment with him tonight . . . In Baghdad.'

10 Artwork and writing: the theme of the supernatural

The following short story is by Saki (whose real name was H.H. Munro), one of the greatest of all English story-tellers. He was born in 1870 and was killed in the Great War in 1916.

Sredni Vashtar

Conradin lives with a cousin, Mrs De Ropp, who seems to derive pleasure from stopping him enjoying himself. Conradin accordingly hates her and has found a secret place where he can escape: a tool-shed at the bottom of the garden, in which he keeps two treasured possessions . . .

In one corner lived a ragged-plumaged Houdan hen, on which the boy lavished an affection that had scarcely another outlet. Further back in the gloom stood a large hutch, divided into two compartments, one of which was fronted with close iron bars. This was the abode of a large polecat-ferret, which a friendly butcher-boy had once smuggled, cage and all, into its present quarters, in exchange for a long-secreted hoard of small silver. Conradin was dreadfully afraid of the lithe, sharp-fanged beast, but it was his most treasured possession. Its very presence in the tool-shed was a secret and fearful joy, to be kept scrupulously from the knowledge of the Woman, as he privately dubbed his cousin. And one day, out of Heaven knows what material, he spun the beast a wonderful name, and from that moment it grew into a god and a religion . . .

. . . Every Thursday, in the dim and musty silence of the tool-shed, he worshipped with mystic and elaborate ceremonial before the wooden hutch where dwelt Sredni Vashtar, the great ferret. Red flowers in their season and scarlet berries in the winter-time were offered at his shrine, for he was a god who laid some special stress on the fierce impatient side of things, as opposed to the Woman's religion, which, as far as Conradin could observe, went to great lengths in the contrary direction. And on great festivals powdered nutmeg was strewn in front of his hutch, an important feature of the offering being that the nutmeg had to be stolen. These festivals were of irregular occurrence, and were chiefly appointed to celebrate some passing event. On one occasion, when Mrs De Ropp suffered from acute toothache for three days, Conradin kept up the festival during the entire three days, and almost succeeded in persuading himself that Sredni Vashtar was personally responsible for the toothache. If the malady had lasted for another day the supply of nutmeg would have given out . . .

. . . After a while Conradin's absorption in the tool-shed began to attract the notice of his guardian. 'It is not good for him to be pottering down there in all weathers,' she promptly decided, and at breakfast one morning she announced that the Houdan hen had been sold and taken away overnight. With her short-sighted eyes she peered at Conradin, waiting for an outbreak of rage and sorrow, which she was ready to rebuke with a flow of excellent precepts and reasoning. But Conradin said nothing: there was nothing to be said. Something perhaps in his white set face gave her a momentary qualm, for at tea that afternoon there was toast on the table, a delicacy which she usually banned on the ground that it was bad for him; also because the making of it 'gave trouble', a deadly offence in the middle-class feminine eye.

'I thought you liked toast,' she exclaimed, with an injured air, observing that he did not touch it.

'Sometimes,' said Conradin.

In the shed that evening there was an innovation in the worship of the hutch-god. Conradin had been wont to chant his praises, tonight he asked a boon.

'Do one thing for me, Sredni Vashtar.'

The thing was not specified. As Sredni Vashtar was a god he must be supposed to know. And choking back a sob as he looked at that other empty corner, Conradin went back to the world he so hated.

And every night, in the welcome darkness of his bedroom, and every evening in the dusk of the tool-shed, Conradin's bitter litany went up: 'Do one thing for me, Sredni Vashtar.'

Mrs de Ropp noticed that the visits to the shed did not cease, and one day she made a further journey of inspection.

'What are you keeping in that locked hutch?' she asked. 'I believe it's guinea-pigs. I'll have them cleared away.'

Conradin shut his lips tight, but the Woman ransacked his bedroom till she found the carefully hidden key, and forthwith marched down to the shed to complete her discovery. It was a cold afternoon, and Conradin had been bidden to come to the house. From the furthest window of the dining-room the door of the shed could just be seen beyond the corner of the shrubbery, and there Conradin stationed himself. He saw the Woman enter, and then he imagined her opening the door of the sacred hutch and peering down with her short-sighted eyes into the thick straw bed where his god lay hidden. Perhaps she would prod at the straw in her clumsy impatience. And Conradin fervently breathed his prayer for the last time. But he knew as he prayed that he did not believe. He knew that the Woman would come out presently with that pursed smile he loathed so well on her face, and that in an hour or two the gardener would carry away his wonderful god, a god no longer, but a simple brown ferret in a hutch. And he knew that the Woman would triumph always as she triumphed now, and that he would grow ever more sickly under her pestering and domineering and superior wisdom, till one day nothing would matter much more with him, and the doctor would be proved right. And in the sting and misery of his defeat, he began to chant loudly and defiantly the hymn of his threatened idol:

Sredni Vashtar went forth,
His thoughts were red thoughts and his teeth were white.
His enemies called for peace, but he brought them death.
Sredni Vashtar the beautiful.

And then of a sudden he stopped his chanting and drew closer to the window-pane. The door of the shed still stood ajar as it had been left, and the minutes were slipping by. They were long minutes, but they slipped by nevertheless. He watched the starlings running and flying in little parties across the lawn; he counted them over and over again, with one eye always on that swinging door. A sour-faced maid came in to lay the table for tea, and still Conradin stood and waited and watched. Hope had crept by inches into his heart, and now a look of triumph began to blaze in his eyes that had only known the wistful patience of defeat. Under his breath, with a furtive exultation, he began once again the paean of victory and devastation. And presently his eyes were rewarded: out through the doorway came a long, low, yellow-and-brown beast, with eyes a-blink at the waning daylight, and dark wet stains around the fur of jaws and throat. Conradin dropped on his knees. The great polecat-ferret made its way down to a small brook at the foot of the garden, drank for a moment, then crossed a little plank bridge and was lost to sight in the bushes. Such was the passing of Sredni Vashtar.

'Tea is ready,' said the sour-faced maid; 'where is the mistress?'

'She went down to the shed some time ago,' said Conradin.

And while the maid went to summon her mistress to tea, Conradin fished a toasting-fork out of the sideboard drawer and proceeded to toast himself a piece of bread. And during the toasting of it and the buttering of it with much butter and the slow enjoyment of eating it, Conradin listened to the noises and silences which fell in quick spasms beyond the dining-room door. The loud foolish screaming of the maid, the answering chorus of wondering ejaculations from the kitchen region, the scuttering footsteps and hurried embassies for outside help, and then, after a lull, the scared sobbings and the shuffling tread of those who bore a heavy burden into the house.

'Whoever will break it to the poor child? I couldn't for the life of me!' exclaimed a shrill voice. And while they debated the matter among themselves, Conradin made himself another piece of toast.

a It is possible to argue that the supernatural is not involved at all in The Signal-Man and The Monkey's Paw, and that everything that happens can be put down to coincidence. Does Saki's story suggest to you that something supernatural has happened, or that the woman's death had no connection with Conradin's prayers to the 'god' Sredni Vashtar?

b Imagine you are producing a film version of Sredni Vashtar. Sketch six frames of a storyboard which would represent six key moments, adding explanatory notes (see page 6). Then write the script for any one scene (such as when they are eating tea).

c Sredni Vashtar would work very well on radio, where we could imagine the events vividly. Write the script for the final few moments (from the point where Mrs De Ropp asks 'What are you keeping in that locked hutch?'), paying particular attention to the use of sound-effects. You might find it helpful to include Mrs De Ropp's or Conradin's thoughts in 'voice over'.